```
ABRACADABRA
ABRACADABR
ABRACADAB
ABRACADA
ABRACAD
ABRACA
ABRAC
ABRA
ABR
AB
A
```

SPRING-HEELED JACK

or

THE TERROR OF LOUISVILLE

PART I

ADVANCE PRAISE FOR

SPRING-HEELED JACK

or

THE TERROR OF LOUISVILLE
PART I

"Reviving the spirit of the popular serial literature of the late 1800s, Ridley Barnett aims to thrill his readers while parsing out a sensational narrative that both entertains and informs. Creatively expanding on old newspaper accounts of bizarre unexplained aerial phenomena over the Ohio River in Louisville, he weaves in real-life events and historical figures to conjure up a believable image of a Victorian river city terrorized by something that comes bounding from above."

~ **David Dominé**, Louisville author of *A Dark Room in Glitter Ball City*

ALSO FROM
NEXT PAGE PUBLISHERS

The Flower is Neutral

A Book of Poetry by Keith Barnett Huff,
Grace Guo, and Ridley Barnett

SPRING-ḣEELED JACK

or

THE TERROR OF LOUISVILLE

PART I

a short story by

RIDLEY BARNETT

NEXT PAGE *PUBLISHERS*
LOUISVILLE, KY
EST 2018

**Spring-heeled Jack or
The Terror of Louisville Part 1** ™
By Keith Barnett Huff
writing as Ridley Barnett

Copyright © 2020 by Keith Barnett Huff.

Published in the United States on July 28th, 2021, by
NEXT PAGE PUBLISHERS LLC.

Cover and book illustrations
by Ridley Barnett Copyright © 2020

Re-edited by Danielle Kent (2023)

Next Page Publishers books may be purchased for
educational, business, or sales promotional use.

*Visit us on the web at **www.nextpagepublishers.com***

Printed in the United States of America
ISBN: **978-1-955665-04-9**

FIRST EDITION

For my grandfather,
Raymond

"The **Kingdom of Heaven** is within *you*; and whosoever shall know *theyself* shall find it."

-ANCIENT KHEMIT PROVERB

.

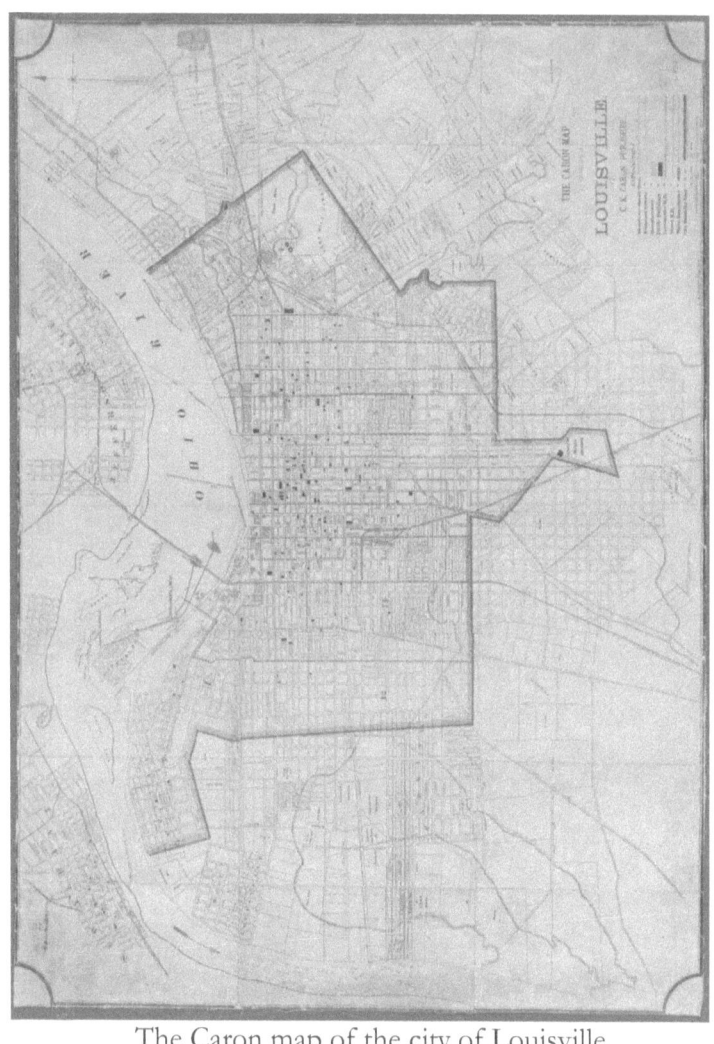

The Caron map of the city of Louisville.
Issued 1880.
Source: https://digitalcollections.nypl.org

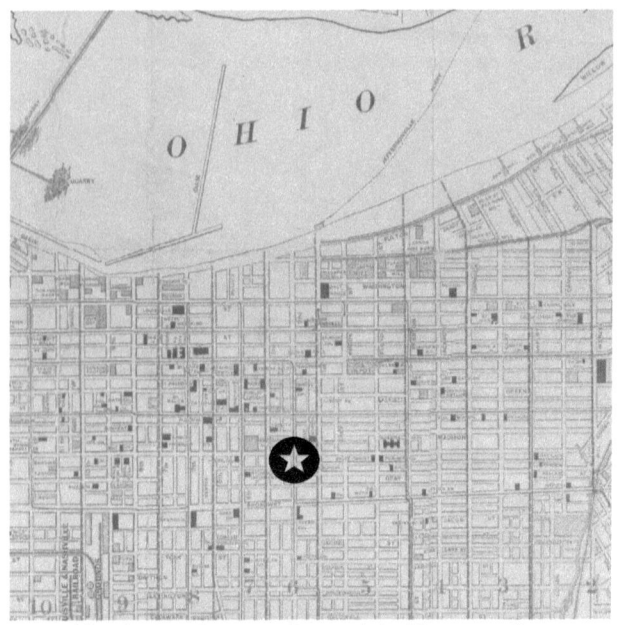

Haddart's Apothecary, Second & Chestnut Streets.

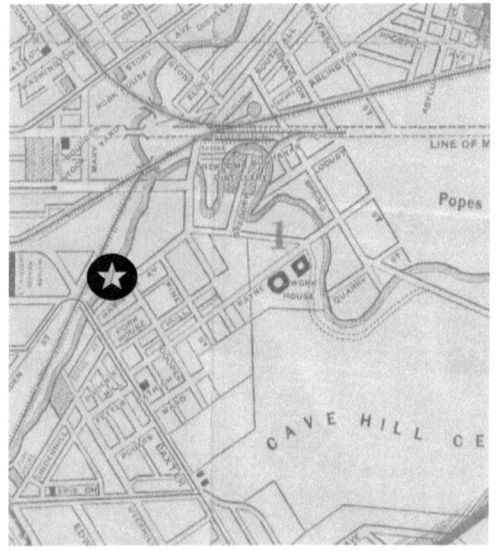

William Quillo's home, Hamilton Avenue.

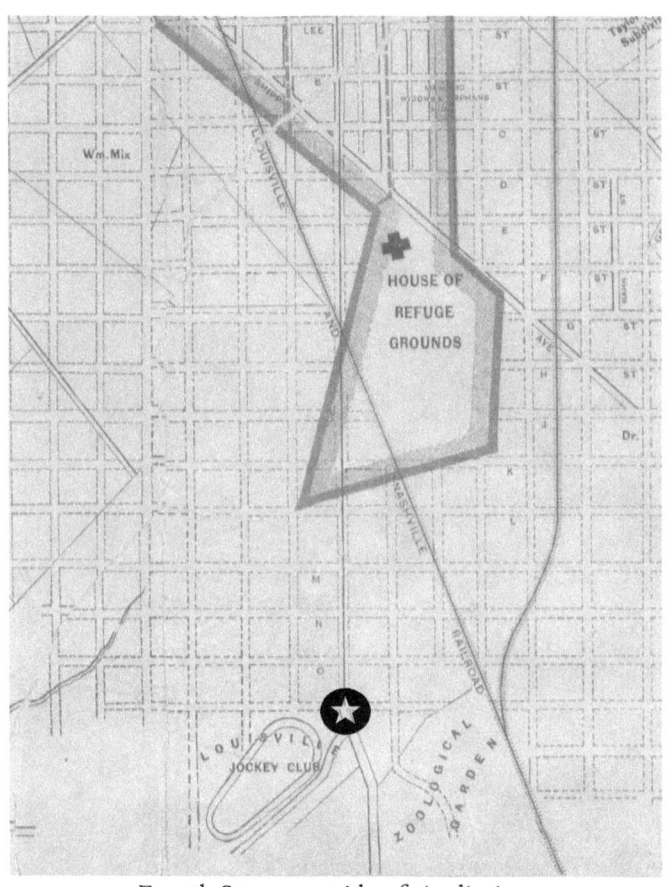

Fourth Street, outside of city limits.

SPRING-HEELED JACK

or

THE TERROR OF LOUISVILLE
PART I

BASED ON TRUE EVENTS

PROLOGUE

FOUND AMONG THE PAPERS OF THE LATE ABBERLINE BINX

"I came from Pandemonium,
If they lay me I'll go back;
Meanwhile round the town I'll jump,
Spring-Heeled Jack."

—ANONYMOUS, *THE PENNY SATIRIST*, 1838

The Ohio River snakes and flows southwest past farmlands, forests, and cities small and large. Not long ago, this waterway served as an extension of the Mason-Dixon Line that divided the United States between free and slave territories.

Six hundred miles down the Ohio River from Pittsburgh is a twenty-six-foot drop known as the Falls of the Ohio, the only obstruction to traffic on the river. Located adjacent to the falls is the Louisville and Portland Canal, where riverboats and barges are raised and lowered to bypass the vertical drop.

High above the canal is the Pennsylvania Railroad Bridge, where a passenger train crosses south from Indiana toward Kentucky. The rear passenger cars pass over narrow channels and exposed limestone ridges of the falls. Just before the treacherous drop, the river widens to a wharf, where steamboats sit moored to the shore lining the riverbank and would announce a city named in honor of the King of France, Louis the XVI.

Louisville—the City of Progress—is sprawled upon the south bank of the Ohio River, a crowded, thriving metropolis of riches and poverty. Five years after the War Between the States ended, the Gilded Age arrived in Louisville, bringing an architectural renaissance. The Derby city saw new libraries, churches, concert halls, post offices, banks, and new courthouse constructed, while private clubs suitable for the wealthiest citizens were within a stone's throw of the busy working poorhouses.

Nearly one millennium of history transformed Louisville from a Native American hunting ground to a stronghold for the Continental Army and eventually into a bustling river town. For a significant period, Louisville was the wild west, a frontier town that many Americans avoided at all costs. Ultimately, the Ohio Valley was tamed by the advent of steamboats, and trains. By the late 1870s, Louisville had become a doorway to the west and a gateway to the south.

The heart of Louisville lies at City Hall. This beautiful Italianate and Second Empire-style building is located on Sixth Street with a front projecting pavilion and an impressive three-level portico. Its most remarkable feature is the 195-foot, four-faced, clock tower with a mansard roof topped by a waving American flag. It is here where all people, poor or wealthy, find a worthy landmark to admire.

On Sixth Street, afternoon traffic is in full swing as mule-drawn buses and horse-drawn carriages bustle through a wave of summer heat. Cyclists cross the intersection under colorful advertisements that work to grab the attention of the public.

A woman cyclist turns on Chestnut Street and moves swiftly around traffic. A massive ad on the side of an apothecary catches her eye.

HADDART'S APOTHECARY
LOCATED AT THE CORNER OF CHESTNUT &
SECOND STREET
WEDNESDAY, JULY 28th, 1880
6:28 P.M.

One advertisement dominates with its large black logo of a watchful Egyptian Eye of Ra painted on the outside brick wall of a drugstore. The ad is for Bu Wizzer Pipe Tobacco.

At the side window two men sip coffee and savor a gentle breeze after suffering through the heat of yet another summer day. The moment of bliss is interrupted when the younger man's attention is caught by a large cigar-shaped object floating high above the Pennsylvania Railroad Bridge. "What is that?" he asks.

The elder gentleman's eyes widen as he sees beyond his young friend's pointing finger. "Looks like a… toy balloon."

The swollen dirigible alters its course and drifts in their direction.

Looking to one another to verify if what they are seeing is real, the men hear a metal whirring sound that echoes across the city.

PROLOGUE

As the gas-filled airship nears less than a block away, the two men make out a propeller in its rear. Suspended under the top cigar-shaped portion is a vessel made of white steel, shaped like the keel of a ship.

Surrounded by machinery, a pilot is dressed in black leather with a silver helmet and goggles, uses his hands and feet to control the rotating mechanism that gives him control over the ship. The aeronaut is seated yet exerts himself to keep the balloon in a horizontal position by swinging his arms to and fro above his head as his feet work double treadles.

The two terrified men watch as the sky is blotted out by the hulking cigar that drifts overhead.

A second passenger materializes from a rear portion of the steel gondola. Dressed in the same attire, the aeronaut leans out to salute the two terrified men.

The elongated balloon cruises south toward Broadway, a street that stretches seven miles from Baxter Avenue on the east to the flowing southern curve of the Ohio River on the west. Broadway is the longest street in the city and serves as a link that transforms from downtown to suburbs with its mix of commercial structures and grand residences.

One such commercial home belongs to Solomon Mason, a New Orleans land developer working on expanding the city further south. His office is temporarily set up inside his mansion, an impressive three-story American Queen Anne, sheathed in pale white wood panels topped with double roofed turrets.

SPRING-HEELED JACK

At the entrance to the courtyard, two guardian sphinxes watch over the private property under the shade of a tulip poplar that adds a sweet fragrance to the air.

CHAPTER ONE

Inside the Mason mansion, Louisville Police Officer William Quillo, a man in his early thirties, is seated in front of a large oak desk. He studies the office. On the far wall, maps display the surrounding area and blueprints for future mansions to be built in Louisville's southern suburbs. Next, his eyes move to a painting of the Boukoleon Palace in Constantinople being raided by Templer Knights during the Fourth Crusade.

The painting felt like an omen. But was it good or bad?

Across the room behind him, seated in leather club chairs, are Solomon's two sons, Hollis, and Israel. Both men concentrate on properly igniting the tips of their cigars.

"Care for one?" Hollis asks in a raspy voice.

"Thanks, but I brought my own," Will says, withdrawing a well-used tobacco pipe from his pocket.

Israel downs a glass of Kentucky bourbon. "Father should be here any second."

Will opens a small leather satchel of tobacco and packs his pipe full. "I could use some timber."

Israel tosses Will a matchbook. "Keep it."

"Thanks," Will says, reading the matchbook cover. The Owl's Nest, Monte Rio, California.

The double doors to the office are thrown open, as Solomon Mason enters. "Hello, boys."

"Father!" the sons reply in unison.

Will stands, but before he can speak, Solomon motions him to sit. "Boys, did you take care of that Metropolitan Theater issue?"

"Yes, father, Mr. Whallen has been delt with," Hollis answers.

"Wonderful! Mr. Quillo, please excuse my lateness. This is our busy time of year. Our mutual friend Detective Sam Burton has informed me that you're a good Protestant lad, and he believes that you would make an outstanding detective."

"Well, that's very kind of him to say."

Solomon, dressed in a blue and white striped seersucker suit, stands tall behind his high-back leather chair. "Your situation is unique." He examines Will for a few seconds and asks, "Your wife is… Catholic?"

"Yes," Will responds, hearing the judgmental tone in the question.

"Irish Catholic!" Solomon adds. "Detective Burton has asked me if I would be willing to pull some strings for you. He says that our chief of police, John Weatherford, is not too keen on Catholics. Nor is he to those who marry outside their denomination."

"No sir, he's not," Will replies. Then, holding Solomon's gaze, Will strikes a match and sucks the flame into his pipe.

Pulling out his chair to sit down, Solomon points toward the front of his home. "No doubt you saw my sign out front?"

Will fans his match out. "You mean the one that reads, Irish need not apply?"

CHAPTER ONE

"What will you do if the Pope decides to invade America? Who will your wife be loyal to?"

"She will be loyal to me. I am loyal to my country."

"Indeed. Well, you're in luck, Mr. Quillo." Solomon folds his hands together in the shape of a triangle. "I have sympathy for my fellow citizens. I do! It's not your wife's fault she was born to a drunken and brutal people. No doubt you have tamed her."

Will grinds his teeth in silent protest.

Solomon retrieves a blood red folder from his desk drawer and opens it. "One thing about me, Mr. Quillo is that I do my research before going into business with anyone."

"I'm not afraid of a background check, Mr. Mason."

"Grand. One item of concern is that you are friendly with the blacks. I know this because my informants have witnessed you in conversation with a certain African American leader, Robert Fox."

Will clears his throat. He chooses his words carefully. "In my profession, the key to solving any crime is gathering information. Be it clues, evidence, or statements. To help me do that I must have connections all over the city. By all types of people. Police Captain Delos Bligh taught me that."

Solomon looks blankly at Will.

Will shifts forward. Solomons neutral stare is difficult to read.

"I suppose you're right." Solomon scans the first page in the folder. "Your family roots, what do you know of them?"

"Sir?" Will asks.

"The Quillo family. They have been in Louisville for a time. You fought for Lincoln in the War Between the States. I will not hold that against you. Your father and mother are deceased. In fact, your father died during the Bloody Monday Riots. Any idea which side he was defending? I do! Ah, I see your family tree goes back to pre-revolutionary times and that they immigrated from England to New Jersey in... 1752. Very impressive."

Will clears his throat. "Oh! Well, I did not know-"

Solomon flips the page and reads further. "Hmm, that is not good. Not good at all!"

"Sir?" Will responds, cracking his neck.

"Your, great grandfather, Trevor Quillo, was a... *Tory.*"

Will's face pales. His grandfather was, in fact, an American colonist who supported the British side during the American Revolution.

Solomon, with a politician's smile, closes Wills' file. "Look son, I know you're a good police officer. Christ, this year alone, you single handily stopped the assassination of Mayor Baxter. And, if that wasn't enough, just this month, you apprehended Louisville's most notorious criminal, John Vonderheide—a man who has committed over forty known burglaries and the heinous crime of murdering a thirteen-year-old girl. If anyone deserves a promotion, it's you. So, that begs the question. How good are your detective skills?"

Will tilts his head to think a moment. "You and your sons just returned from California."

CHAPTER ONE

Solomon's eyes widen. "Yes, how did you know that?"

Will holds up the box of matches. "The Owls Nest Café, Monte Rio, California."

"Lucky guess."

"While there, you stayed at Bohemian Grove."

Solomon leans back as his mouth falls open.

His sons shift uncomfortably in their chairs.

"How did you know—"

"The *Courier* wrote an article describing how the rich and powerful of this nation gather there every mid-July."

"How can you be so sure we belong?"

"Why else would you be in Monte Rio in mid-July?"

"Damn that Henry Watterson and his newspaper! All right, Mr. Quillo, you appear to be a calm and clever lad. With your current police record, I would bet the family farm you're on par to be the next Delos Bligh." Solomon pauses to laugh.

Will gives Solomon a sly smile.

"I will overlook your ancestor's mistake and your wife's background. Also, I consider who knows who in this city. Lucky for you, being friends with Jonathan Webb has its perks. So, I will help you."

For the first time today, Will relaxes.

"First things first, I'm going to need you to do me a favor." Solomon says.

"What sort of favor?" Will says tightening back up.

Solomon bites his lip. "Ah, it seems that Mr. Burton, your superior, did not inform you. You see I have several officers on the force who… help my family out."

"What sort of help?"

Solomon leans forward. "Whatever I need! Whatever I want!"

Will's eyes move to the painting of the raided palace in Constantinople. "Mr. Solomon, I'm afraid I'm going to have to turn down your offer."

Solomon's gaze moves to his sons as if to communicate a secret. "How disappointing."

Will stands to straighten his navy-blue police jacket. "Gentlemen, thank you for your time. Unfortunately, I need to be going. I'm on duty tonight. My apologies for taking up your time."

Hollis and Israel stand out of respect.

"Oh, Mr. Quillo!" Solomon says. His stare intensifies. "Just out of curiosity, why come to me? Why not go to Mayor Baxter? I mean… the man owes you a favor."

"I have… already exhausted that favor."

"Hmm. I hope it was worth it. Because unless you can find a little *gold* to bribe your way in, I am now the only man in this city who can make you a detective."

Not sure what Solomon means, Will secures his pith helmet to his head. "Good day, gentlemen."

Down the hall is Detective Sam Burton, a short, heavy-set man. He draws a substantial drag from his cigar. Seeing Will exit the office, he moves up the hall to greet his friend. "Will! How did it go?"

Will's fists ball up at the sight of his superior. His ears become noticeably hot.

CHAPTER ONE

"What?" Burton asks, seeing the look on his friend's face.

Will stops in front of him. "The Masons are a damn crime family, and you have pledged yourself to them?"

Burton pulls Will to the side. "Will, the Masons will one day own this city. Jesus, pal, who do you think was behind the assassination attempt of the mayor? Will, I'm doing you a favor!"

"Wow, wait a minute. Sam Redd was going to kill Baxter because he was discharged for drunkenness."

"No, Will. They pushed him to do it. He was motivated by that sure. But he was—"
"Burton! What possibly made you think I would accept Solomon's offer?"

"Will, I know you. We served together. I know what you did in the war and…"

Will scoffs and pushes past Burton to head quickly down a grand staircase. "That was *war*!"

"Look, I'm sorry. You know this is the only way you're going to make detective." Burton watches as Will disappears to the lower levels of the house.

"Oh, Mr. Burton!" Israel calls out while moving quickly down the hall followed by his brother.

Burton turns to address the two brothers. "Hey! I… I was just coming to see you."

Israel pushes a sharp finger into Burton's chest. "Mr. Quillo will be a problem."

"Oh?" Burton says, wide-eyed.

"Mr. Quillo is a smart man," Hollis says through a thick cloud of tobacco smoke.

Burton coughs as Hollis steps closer. "The last thing we need is a *good boy* meddling in our affairs." In a quiet, confident voice, he commands, "Take Mr. Quillo to meet his maker."

Visibly sweating, Burton answers, "Yes! Yes sir, Mr. Mason."

Outside, Will exits the property through an arbor and out onto the sidewalk of Broadway, where he is suddenly caught in a stampede of people. He is shoved back and forth as fearful pedestrians move around him, looking to the air and pointing in disbelief.

Will follows their gaze toward a loud mechanical screeching. Above them a cigar-shaped object drifts overhead. Will's mouth falls open as the shadow of the flying machine consumes him.

His pipe crashes to the ground, spilling out all its hot tobacco.

Is this real? Will observes his surroundings: men and women are at their windows, pointing at the craft with a look of wondrous awe.

A horse-drawn carriage crashes on the sidewalk as both driver and horse are distracted by the mysterious craft.

"Will!" someone shouted.

Looking around to see who is calling for him, Will sees his longtime friend Robert Fox, a sixty-three-year-old African American. Fox was made famous when in 1870 he entered a segregated streetcar to stage a protest with his brother and their friend. In 1871 they won their case and helped to desegregate Louisville's streetcars. A first in the United States history.

"Will, what is that?" Robert asks.

CHAPTER ONE

"I... I don't know. A big damn balloon!"

Robert claps Will on the back. "Come on. We can get a better look up on the roof."

Will follows Robert across the street weaving through bewildered pedestrians to a three-story boarding house. Both men charge up the fire escape. On the roof, sweat drips from Will's face as he breaths in short gasps. He walks along the roof to the southern side of the building, where the flying machine should be visible.

Nothing.

Looking south, both men search an empty sky. Below them they see brick and stone mansions that thin out into rural countryside.

"Where the hell is it?" Robert asks.

"Look!" Will shouts.

Ascending at a tilt from Central Park, a private estate opened to the public, the giant cigar rises back above the tree line and slowly rotates south to continue onward.

Both men watch as the phantom craft cruises just above the tree line until it is hidden from view by the dense wild forest miles away.

The sound of the ship's screeching propeller fades away, only to be replaced by the tolling of church bells that ring out across the river city.

CHAPTER TWO

As the event comes to an end with no explanation, word spreads by telegraph wires, couriers, and telephones. Apothecaries, police stations, and fire stations are bombarded with cries of worried and curious citizens.

Within the hour young newspaper couriers race to deliver the evening press to customers who are already lined up and waiting. The local press has added a hastily put together special front page for the evening newspaper.

A Sixteenth Street paperboy cries out, "Read all about it! Railroad man witnesses flying machine!"

On the north-east corner of Fourth and Broadway, a paperboy cries out, "Farmer not far from the Louisville Jockey Club witnesses flying machine!" The twelve-year-old paperboy is standing outside of Slogan's Confectionery, a popular location in the city, as concerned citizens swarm him to buy a copy of the special late edition.

Just to the right of the three-story, brownstone-front confectionary is an elderly redheaded woman who plays a hammered dulcimer. She uses her two small spoon-shaped mallet hammers to strike out the melody to the song "Simple Gifts" by Shaker Elder Joseph Brackett.

CHAPTER TWO

Will and Robert stand at the corner with their friend Ed Loudermilk, thirty-seven and goofy looking.

The tall dirty-blonde haired Loudermilk is wearing a sandwich advertisement board over his body. The front and back of the ad reads: "COLGAN'S TAFFY TOLU - WORLD'S FIRST FLAVORD CHEWING GUM - MANUFACTURED IN LOUISVILLE."

Loudermilk rattles a glass jar full of loose white square pieces of gum. "*Get your free sample!*" He yells at people as they hurry past. To Will and Robert, he says, "So, every night my wife comes to bed ... *Get your free sample!* Right when I'm about to doze off, she wants to discuss what *I* did wrong that day. *First ever flavored gum samples!* Can you believe that? Do your wives do that to you fellers too? *Free samples!*"

"Loudermilk, can you please knock that off?" Robert demands.

"What?"

"Stop yelling your pitch mid-sentence while you're talking to us," Will barks.

"Sorry," Loudermilk says with a sour face, "I'm working here."

Robert places a supportive hand on Loudermilk's shoulder. "Son, you work as a firefighter during the day and sell candy here in the evening. When does your wife ever get time to see you to critique you?"

"Will, how was your meeting with Solomon Mason?" Loudermilk asks, ignoring Robert's question as he continues to rattle gum at passing pedestrians.

Will pauses to think. "I need to study their proposal."

"What's there to study? They can either help you or they can't." Robert says.

"The Mason's come with some… obligations."

"Will, I know you want to become a detective not just because of job security. You have a gift." Robert says.

"Hold it. What do you mean job security? *Free samples!*"

"An election year is coming up." Will's eyes are bolted on a line of coffins for sale by a street vendor across Broadway. "If Mayor Baxter loses, I'm out of a job. The entire police force is out of a job. I'll be back at the wharf working as a night watchman."

"Ah, that's right. Every time a new administration takes office, y'all get the boot!" Loudermilk says scratching his chin.

"Except for the detectives! They get to keep their jobs," Robert reminds him.

Loudermilk withdraws a silver flask. He offers it to Robert and Will.

Both men decline.

Loudermilk empties the hot liquor down his throat and finishes by giving a sigh of orgasmic satisfaction.

"What are you going to tell Mary?" Robert asks.

"I'm not going to say anything. I don't want to worry her."

The three men stand in silence. They watch as the paperboy sells the last of the late edition.

Robert shakes his head. "It's been a rough couple of years for us black folk. Those Southern Redeemer's have been unraveling all the work we have achieved in

17

the last ten years for equality." Robert locks eyes with Will. "The Masons are dangerous. Want to know why? Word on the street is the Masons are in cahoots with the Jacobs administration."

"How so?" Will asks.

"Certain individuals within the administration want to make Hollis Mason the Chief of Police. Will, they're coming for the police. Won't be long till their reach spreads like a cancer to all other branches of the government. You might lose a job, but we blacks are going to lose our progress. I say... Stand and fight!"

Will pauses to reflect on this new information. He folds his copy of the late edition under his arm. "I need to get home for dinner. My shift begins in a few hours." He tips his helmet to his friends.

"Ah, heck. Don't give up. Hey! On the house." Loudermilk holds up the jar of gum to Will. "Free samples?"

Will holds out his hand and watches as tiny white squares cover his palm. "Thanks fellas. See y'all around." He places the gum in his pocket. Before saddling his horse, he places a coin into the elder dulcimer's donation jar.

"Opportunity is coming my friend. Just you wait. Good always prevails," Robert yells to Will as he rides away.

CHAPTER THREE

IRISH HILL NEIGHBORHOOD
8:11 P.M.

East Broadway ends at Baxter Avenue by the main entrance to the prominent Cave Hill Cemetery, a burying ground for the city's most prolific citizens. To the north of the cemetery is a small neighborhood tucked between Phoenix Hill and Butchertown called Irish Hill and is home to the city's Irish immigrants.

The most significant landmark in Irish Hill is the newly built city workhouse, a brick and stone castle-like prison. The fortress sits upon a hill and looms over the Catholic community. Louisville's largest watershed, Beargrass Creek, runs through the vicinity, carrying the dumped animal waste from Butchertown's slaughter-houses. The citizens of this district must also live with the constant smell of fermenting mash that lingers from the neighboring breweries and bourbon distilleries of Phoenix Hill.

On Hamilton Avenue, one of just a few noncommercial areas in Irish Hill, sit rows of shotgun cottages that line both sides of the street. The first of these homes has a plot of ground where herbs, fruits, flowers, and vegetables wait to be harvested. The rear of the cottage overlooks Beargrass Creek and the Louisville skyline.

CHAPTER THREE

Inside the cottage, Will places a copy of the *Courier-Journal* on his kitchen table. "It would appear that the closing ceremony of the du Pont Conservatory has been replaced!"

His wife, Mary, rushes to his side. The newspaper's late edition insert page headline reads, "Mystery That Is Holding the City in Awe!" Mary's hands caress the paper like a sacred manuscript. "You saw it?" she asks, eyes wide with curiosity.

"Flew right over me!" Will says, pushing a lock of red hair behind her ear.

"Oh, how I wish I could have seen it."

"It's odd, though." Will ate the last of his Kentucky burgoo before continuing. "Why did it not stop?" He retrieves a handful of soda crackers from a tin box. "If I'd invented something like that, I'd want to show it off. Get famous or something."

Mary moves out to the living room and sits in her red apple colored armchair. "It's like a hot air balloon! But this is far more elaborate."

"I reckon it's a new type of Ritchel dirigible."

"What is that?" Mary asks.

Will put his bowl down and moves to a bookshelf containing old issues of *Harper's Weekly*. His index finger brushes past the spines of each volume until he withdraws an issue and hands it off to his wife.

Mary marvels at the black and white illustration of a man sitting on a brass frame no bigger than a rowboat. The brass frame hangs beneath a cylindrical rubber gas bag and together allows the aeronaut to fly high above Boston Common. "Saturday, July 13, 1878. The new flying machine!" Mary reads off the cover.

"The man you see is aeronaut, Mark Quindlen. The dirigible he is flying is designed by American inventor Professor Charles Ritchel. He called his machine the Dirigicycle."

Mary compares the illustrations of the two airships. She looks up at Will. "Today's is no Dirigicycle, it's a Didirigiship!"

"It's certainly a marvel to behold."

"Do you think the airship today was piloted by Quindlen and Ritchel?"

Will clicks his tongue. "My gut tells me no. Ritchel and Quindlen earned a living by giving aerial shows."

Mary opens the magazine. She thumbs through the pages until she finds the cover article.

Will picks up his empty soup bowl and carries it into the kitchen. The smell of fresh paint seizes his nose. He places his bowl in the sink before following the chemical odor to the guest room.

Inside, he discovers not only a fresh coat of yellow paint on the walls but also an empty baby's crib, furnishings, and a rocking chair bunched together in the center of the room. Alarmed, Will closes the door softly. He inhales deeply and turns to walk back to the living room. "Mary, why did you paint the guest room?"

His wife does not make eye contact. Instead, she folds the paper neatly and places it between the red cushions and stares blankly ahead. "Well… we bought the paint. Why waste it?"

"And the crib?"

CHAPTER THREE

She places a finger on her upper lip. "I just wanted to see how it would have… looked."

Will moves closer to her. "It's been over a month. You *have* to move on."

Mary is on top of Will now, shouting, "I'm not like you. I can't just *move on*. I miss my baby!"

Will snorted a scornful, dismissive laugh, "So do I."

"It would do my soul good to see a wee bit of sadness from you. Sadness for our dead son!"

"*Enough!*"

"I want a divorce."

"Awe, here we go!"

"You're a cold, cold man, William Quillo. How dare you command me to move on."

"Why is it, every time we argue you default to… to a divorce. I thought you Catholics were against divorce?"

"Seeing as how my family, and my church has already disavowed me for marrying *you*, I have nothing else left to lose."

Will's fists ball up. "Neither do I."

Mary's deep green eyes pierce his. "Pray with me?"

"No," he protests.

"William?"

Will relaxes. He stares deeply into his wife's eyes and softly replies, "Mary, I'm not having this discussion."

Mary removes her rosary and places a warm touch on his cold shoulders. "Don't walk away from God, Will."

Will folds Mary's arms to her side. "Stop! *Stop*. Mary… I'm all… prayed out."

"William!"

Will takes two steps backward. "I'm sorry, Mary."

"What is it?"

"I thought being a good man was enough to get through this life. I have always tried to do what I thought was right. I just have this... hole in my heart."

Both their expressions are touched with confusion. Will continues. "A hole that has been there for a long time! I don't know how to... to fill it." Will stares into Mary's eyes, looking for judgment. Instead, he sees understanding.

"Will, you never *really* told me anything about your past. About the war or your childhood. The only clues I have are the nights you wake screaming or crying. Or both."

"You don't want to hear those stories."

"Yes, I do."

"We are not to discuss these things *ever* again. Do you understand?"

"Do you want a divorce? Yes, or no?" She asks casually.

Neither one of them speak.

A knock at the front door brings them both back to reality.

Will answers the door to find Burton off to the side with his hands in his pockets smoking a cigarillo.

"What are you doing here?" Will asks.

"Your shift starts now. There was a robbery... At the Masons' house."

"Robbery?"

CHAPTER THREE

"Might be a good opportunity to square things away between you and Mr. Mason."

Mary comes to the door. "Fáilte, Sam. Can I get you something to drink?"

"No thanks, Mary. I'm fine." Burton looks to Will. "Will, we need to go. Now!"

Mary walks to a side table and picks up Will's pith helmet, utility belt, and a small brass lantern clip-on. She walks back to Will who is already re-buttoning his blue uniform jacket.

When he finishes dressing, Will grabs Mary's hand and gives it a squeeze. "Before I go, I want you to know that my answer is no."

"Watch over my husband, Mr. Burton." Mary demands as she gives Will a reserved gaze.

Burton stares off into the distance and nods his head, taking the last drag of his cigarillo before flicking it away.

CHAPTER FOUR

Will follows Burton through the servant's side entrance of the Mason's house. In the servant's foyer, Will sees an elderly maid talking with a young officer.

"I came into the room and found it… a mess," the maid said shaking, "When I looked out the broken window, I saw… across the street someone or… *something* leaping onto the neighbors' roof!"

The young officer pauses to look up from his notes. "Ma'am, did you mean leaping roof to roof?"

"No! From street to roof!"

"Street to roof?" The officer says back confused.

"See, I told you this is important," Burton says, leading Will into the main hall where a chandelier sways from the echoing yells of the home's master.

Solomon Mason moves across his library like a dog claiming its territory. "Yes. I am missing something *very* important to me."

A detective waits to jot down any helpful details Solomon manages to bark at him.

Solomon continues, "It is an item I just brought back from my trip. It is an ancient relic. Where is Delos? I want Delos Bligh! He's the only detective fit for this search!" Solomon stops when he sees across the hall Officer William Quillo alive and well peeking into his antiquarian room.

CHAPTER FOUR

Will studies the strange and exotic array of ancient Egyptian paraphernalia. The room consists of a ceiling painted blue with gold five-pointed gold stars, display cases that hold an array of Egyptian artifacts. A side window is broken-in and covered over by a white sheet. At the center of the chamber is a lone display case shattered to pieces.

Burton joins Will, standing beside him. "Solomon is acting too high for his nut. Maybe a night on Green Street with a couple of soiled doves can raise his spirits."

"Come with me," Will commands.

Burton and Will exit the front of the house and move onto the sidewalk. Both men strike a match to light their tobacco. On the street, a sprinkling cart hauling a sizeable wooden cask passes.

A canvas advertisement for Bu Wizzer Pipe Tobacco is stretched over the water cask. The ad once again shows the iconic logo of Ra's black Eye but with the added text that reassures readers that: "THE GODS ALL AGREE BU WIZZER IS THE BEST."

Two protruding pipes from the cask spray river water onto the dirt road to prevent dust from rising in the wind and blowing into the open windows of the beautiful homes that line the street.

Will watches as the cart passes. His gaze is fixed on the watchful eye that stares back at him. "The flying machine, it comes into our city, creates a spectacle, and disappears. Why?" He darts a glance at Burton. "I think it dropped someone off."

Burton shrugs.

"Hours later, Solomon is burglarized?"

"You think it was the flying men?" Burton looks at his master's house with new curiosity. "What do we do now?"

"I'm going to the Louisville Jockey Club."

"Why?"

"Because that's where the flying ship was last seen. Near the racetrack. If I had a flying machine and needed to hide it, that's where I would hide it. Wait until dark, circle back and land it right in the center of the racing field! There's nothing around for miles but farmland and woods. The thief is most likely on his way there now."

"The last race of the day was at five o'clock," Burton adds.

"The ship arrived in Louisville sometime after seven."

"You know you will have to pass the House of Refuge to get to the racetrack, right?"

"I'll be fine."

"What if you get the vapors?"

"I said I'll be fine!" Will empties his pipe and stuffs it into his coat, "Find the chief and convince him to bring a patrol through there. Have him issue arms."

Burton points his thumb at his chest. "Wait just a minute, I'm the detective. You go fetch the—"

Will grabs Burton by the collar and shoves him backward into a lamp post. "*You owe me!*"

Burtons' muscles tense by the sudden brute force. "All right! All right!"

"Give me your piece," Will demands, releasing his pudgy superior.

27

CHAPTER FOUR

Burton withdraws an Adams revolver and surrenders it hilt-side up.

Will takes the grey steel gun and checks for ammunition. He holsters the gun in his trousers and mounts his horse. Then, with a swift kick to drive the horse forward, man and steed take off west across Broadway.

Burton turns to see Solomon watching from his front porch. He looks down to his feet and bites his lip. Then, taking a deep breath, he looks back up at Solomon, who continues to watch him with the look of a disappointed father. Burton removes a second pistol from his back holster, checks it for ammunition, and mounts his horse. Taking a deep breath, he knows what he must do.

Solomon closes his front door. He hurries into the main hallway where his son Hollis is escorting the last detectives out the side servant's door.

Israel strikes a match and lights his cigar. "Well, now what do we do?"

Solomon moves across the hall and into the Egyptian room.

His obedient sons follow.

Solomon walks over broken glass and past three golden Egyptian masks displayed on top of a mantle above a stone-carved fireplace. Above the masks is a shield with a Confederate crest.

Next to a life-size statue of Ptah, an ancient Egyptian masonry deity, Solomon opens an oak cabinet that holds an array of guns and melee weapons.

Solomon withdraws a rifle and tosses one to each of his sons. "We are going to get that relic back."

"How?" Hollis asks, "We don't even know where to begin to look."

Solomon withdraws a box of bullets from a drawer in the oak cabinet. "Mr. Quillo has a hunch! He believes the thief is heading to the Jockey Club."

"Perhaps he'll place a bet," Hollis jokes.

"He's a bit late for the Derby!" Israel adds.

"We should call the rest of the Brotherhood for help!" Hollis suggests.

"No! There's no time! Besides, we can handle this ourselves," Solomon says, pumping the lever of his Winchester rifle.

CHAPTER FIVE

"The world is not prepared yet to understand the philosophy of Occult Sciences— let them assure themselves first of all that there are beings in an invisible world, whether 'Spirits' of the dead or elementals; and that there are hidden powers in man, which are capable of making a God of him on earth."

—H. P. BLAVATSKY (1831-1891)

BROADWAY AT THIRD STREET CROSSING
8:59 P.M.

The final rays of sunlight set the color of the sky an unnatural shade of crimson. Black smoke rises to the heavens from hundreds of chimneys. The prospect of a new flying machine has the city energized as couples are out enjoying a late-night promenade. The sounds of music pour out from an Edison phonograph set up at the intersection. An elderly woman and her grandchild manage the device. They sit and watch as the couples stroll to the song "Ah! May the Red Rose Live Alway" by Stephen Foster.

Broadway and Third Street's homes consist of either brick or carved stone surrounded by black wrought iron fences. Third street's nickname is "Millionaires Row" and is where all the wealthiest of Louisville reside. The sidewalks here are double in size for promenading. Its road is covered in wooden squares for easy travel, and even the air is fragranced by the sweet smells of serviceberries, magnolias, and tulip poplars.

Still in a grievous mood, William Quillo halts his horse at Third Street crossing to wait for crossing traffic. Will calculates the distance and time he needs to get to the Jockey Club. If his hunch was correct, the thief was already there, and his efforts would be fruitless. He watches impatiently for the traffic light to rotate to green.

Across the city, bells toll for the nine o'clock hour.

Inside a nearby mansion, a father and son, dressed in their night gowns and robes, play a round of late-night chess. They are surrounded by an enclave of books. A hand-blown stain glass windowpane is open, allowing a gentle cool breeze to enter along with the melodies of Mr. Foster.

Beside the window is a birdcage built to look like a miniature replica of the mansion. Inside, a red cardinal is perched, chirping away peacefully.

Just then, the cardinal flutters around frantically as its chirping grows to a higher pitch.

The father and son turn in their seats to see the bird violently hitting every bar in the cage as it searches for a way out.

"What's wrong, Paw?"

An odd feeling of being watched causes Will to instinctively look to a three-story mansion across the street. Will sees a black figure leap to the roof of the estate. The figure comes to rest upon a turret, perched like a gargoyle.

Will's gaze brakes when pedestrians crossing to the other side startles his horse. After calming his steed, Will searches for the specter.

The phantom's head rotates around. Beady red eyes stare back at him, sending a shiver down his spine.

A blue orb materializes on the specter's chest, followed by a roar so loud it threatens to break Will's lucidity.

In a single bound, the phantom leaps to the middle of the Third Street crossing.

A row of streetlamps flicker enough light to reveal the unsettling sight of a thin figure dressed in black leather and a silver helmet, its face contoured with long pointed ears and two devilish horns protruding from its forehead.

The half-man, half-demon, gives a high-pitched laugh as the blue orb on the creature's chest begins vomiting flames.

Pedestrians see the demon and flee, convinced that the devil himself has arrived.

Unholstering his revolver, Will digs his heels into his horse. The mare ignites into a full gallop after the demon.

The creature leaps sideways down Third Street fifty yards, sailing over a moving carriage.

The coachman is caught by surprise and crashes on the sidewalk. Mass, momentum, and the weight of the passengers cause the carriage to overturn.

Will avoids the skidding carriage and aims his revolver, looking for a clean shot.

Frightened pedestrians watch as the demon bounds down South-Third like a man who has just lost all sense of proprieties.

Ahead of the demon leaper two mounted officers ride towards him, blowing their alarm whistles. But the high-pitched notes do nothing to stop the specter.

With a forward leap and an audible crazed laugh, the creature sails between them, clubbing both men off their horses.

Will watches in awe as the demon sways off lamp posts and tree limbs with superhuman ability. He follows as fast as he can, dodging the crashed cyclists and terrified pedestrians. Then, with a clear shot, Will aims and fires two rounds at the demon leaper.

Aware of the bullets zipping past him, the creature skids to a stop. It turns to face a three-story red-stone mansion and springs onto the roof before disappearing over the other side.

Will sees this and follows by crossing west on St. Catharine Street. He rides past Fourth Street. Not seeing the beast anywhere causes him to panic. *Did I lose it?* His intuition is telling him to turn south on Fifth Street. Moving south on Fifth stops he sees a dark specter leaping through the forest.

The demon reaches the next intersection where the homes here are country estates and possess vast land with large trees that spread a thick canopy of green leaves.

CHAPTER FIVE

The demon leaper continues to bound through the forest estates.

Will, losing sight of the jumping freak, rides as fast as his steed will carry him; but it is no use as each bound sends the demon farther and farther away.

At the next intersection is Central Park's entrance with its closed gatehouse used for collecting a ten-cent entrance fee. The gate faces north toward Fifth Street and Weisinger Avenue.

Will sees up ahead heavy traffic of farm wagons and mule cars passing both east and west on Weisinger Avenue. Moving north up Fourth Street is a tired mule pulling a loaded streetcar full of equally exhausted house servants.

With a single bound, the demon lands atop the streetcar and leaps again across Weisinger Avenue, cleaning a tall hay wagon, and lands on the roof of the gatehouse on the other side. The creature turns to sneer at Will. "Ta-ta!" the pale demon yells.

A belch of blue fire lights up the entire intersection, followed by a howling roar.

Will is blinded by the blue light. His teeth rattle like dice inside his skull at the sound of the demonic roar. By the time he regains his sight, the creature has vanished.

Silver clouds shroud the crescent moon as the demon leaper clears over the top of a fifty-four-foot-long wooden arbor used in the summertime as an ice-cream saloon. He continues to spring south through Central Park.

SPRING-HEELED JACK

This recreational property is beautifully landscaped with a spider web of curving walking paths. The dense forest opens to expose a pond for romantic paddleboat excursions. At the shore is a white gazebo and dock that moors rowing boats. Further into the park a house is surrounded by 18-acres of bucolic scenery. The country home sits upon a commanding knoll. This is the du Pont mansion.

In the 1850s, two brothers from Delaware, Alfred Victor and Biederman du Pont, moved to Louisville to start several enterprises. They would become the wealthiest men in the Derby city owning a paper mill, Central Passenger Railway Co in Louisville, and several iron, coal, and steel companies. To escape the noisy and tumultuous life of downtown the brothers bought the country villa to surrender themselves to all the leisure and calm that the countryside has to offer.

The demon sees the lone residence silhouetted against the darkness of the forest with its windows glowing a soft yellow. The tall thin demon lands in the front yard of the brick Italianate home and immediately propels himself to its roof. He walks to the other side of the villa breathing heavily. Then, the demon stops and stands like a statue. A devilish grin fills his face as the creature breaths in the warm night air, taking a moment to listen to the symphony of chaos he just finished conducting. Once satisfied, he leaps onward into the darkness of the Louisville Eden.

Further back in the park a giant building will provide the demon a chance to navigate toward the correct direction. "Tally-ho!" cries the demon leaper.

CHAPTER FIVE

High up in the air, the specter falls back down to land on its roof.

The moon, half-faced, emerges from a veil of clouds with enough radiance to reveal a building that is glossy and see-through.

The creature's muscles tense as it realizes the building is a conservatory. He breaks through a glass panel striking his head on an arch support beam and falls to a floral garden below.

After lying motionless for a moment, the demon leaper rolls over on his back, coughing up blood, fighting to suppress the pain that ensnares his whole body. Every movement he makes brings unbearable agony. He stares up at his entry hole, cursing the room's beauty as it glows from the moon rays beaming down.

CHAPTER SIX

Will stands behind the bars of Central Park's double gate entrance. He shakes the cold black iron barrier trying to open it.

Nothing.

He pauses to consider whether he should follow the creature through the park or head down Fourth Street straight for the racetrack. He withdraws his sidearm, shoots the lock and pushes the gates wide open. Will climbs back up on his horse and enters the heavily forested private property.

Long before the Southern Expansion reached what is now Central Park, locals knew that witches and gypsies camped here. During the day they would trade their wares. But by night they danced around fires casting spells in the name of old gods and goddesses.

Will rides through the park using the trails as his guide. Pistol at the ready, he passes the du Pont mansion. He sees up ahead a wide clearing emerge where an imposing 90-foot-tall palm dome conservatory sits bathed in holy moonlight.

A blue light flashes inside the elegant greenhouse.

Will pulls back on the reins of his horse. The stillness of the moment allows him time to feel his heart beating harder than a Viking war drum.

CHAPTER SIX

He kicks his horse on its side, taking off down the hill toward the glass palace.

CHAPTER SEVEN

Sweat rolls down Burton's face as he rides down Third Street. He moves through a neighborhood that is recovering from the shock of a dreadful assault.

Frightened homeowners, such as the father and son who abandoned their game of chess for the show outside, stand at their thresholds recounting their personal experiences of the violent rampage with other neighbors.

Burton, rides by a police officer taking statements from terrified pedestrians. He overhears a wealthy elderly man say, "I saw the devil attack a woman. Tore her clothes right off!"

A young lady says, "He had red eyes! Bulging red eyes! And long fingers sharp as knives."

An elderly woman shrieks, "It was the devil himself! It was the devil himself! Bat wings and all!"

Burton arrives at the gates to Central Park where an officer stands watch. He notices the gates are wide open.

The shrills of police whistles blare out from another street over.

"Hell of a day! Huh, Mr. Burton?" The officer says.

"You posted here?"

"Yup! Eyewitnesses say they saw the... whatever it was enter the park. We're setting up a perimeter now."

"Anyone alert the du Pont's?

"Not sure. But Officer Quillo was seen chasing the maniac. Not sure where he is now."

"I'll watch over the du Pont's. See to the Fifth Street crossing mess."

The officer nods and heads toward the shrills.

After the officer vanishes, Burton proceeds into the park.

CHAPTER EIGHT

Looking through a pane of glass, Will studies the enclosed garden, with its interior teeming with various species of plants and flowers.

Gathering his courage, Will withdraws his pistol and enters. The aroma of wet soil quickly fills his nose. He moves to a nearby horseshoe-shaped oak desk. Behind the desk, he finds a panel of levers. He pulls them backward, causing a row of gas lamps to hiss to life.

A glow of light gradually intensifies revealing remnants of Louisville's centennial celebration. Red, white, and blue bunting drapes every column with an enormous American flag that suspends from the ceiling centered with the entrance.

"Help… *cough*… help!" cries a desperate voice.

Will holds his pistol outstretched, scanning the 100-foot-wide greenhouse. Hundreds of species of plants and flowers block his view. A strong wind blows in from an open portion of the ceiling high above.

Crunch!

Will pauses to curse the noisy gravel path. He clutches his revolver nervously and proceeds off the trail with haste through a grove of banana trees. Several feet away he discovers a discarded silver helmet covered in blood, followed by a red blood trail that leads to a strange device with shoulder straps.

Squatting down, Will picks it up but immediately drops it as it is scalding hot. The blood trail continues to a large fountain at the center of the glass structure.

Will cautiously moves around the fountain to discover a thin pale faced being in a black leather suit. It sits with its back against the fountain.

"Stay where you are! Just… stay!" Will commands.

The demon's pale face looks up at him with pleading blue eyes. It coughs up red blood before waving an open hand.

"Who are you?" Will asks, horrified.

"Please… help me," the creature says in a British accent.

"What… what are you? Why are you here? What *are* you?"

"My name is, Olvilvicera, and I'm here for this." The creature spits blood before he holds up a small gold chest with Egyptian hieroglyphs.

Will edges closer to the wounded creature. "That is one hell of a name!" He points to the gold box. "You… you steal that from Solomon Mason?"

Olvilvicera nods. "The Masons are dangerous. They are part of a secret brotherhood that plans to bring about world chaos."

Will steps forward. "First, I need another name to call you. Second, I know the Masons are dangerous, but what do you mean world chaos?"

"Please! I must get to my airship, the *Aquila*, before midnight. It will depart at Midnight! I cannot let this chest fall into the hands of the Brotherhood of Khonsu. No matter what, you must promise me this chest… ah!" In all his excitement, the demon leaper chafes his wounds.

Will takes off his pith helmet, throws it to the ground, and holsters his revolver in his pants pocket. He unbuttons his jacket and strips it off. "You look awful. If! If I am to help you, I cannot move you until your wounds are sorted out." Will withdraws a pocketknife.

"Thank you! Thank you! You can call me… Jack."

Will kneels to examine Jack's legs. "Jack? That is a whole lot easier. My name is Officer William Quillo."

"Thank you for trusting me."

"I don't. Try anything foolish, and I will kill you."

The wounded creature relaxes and nods in agreement.

CHAPTER NINE

Across the lake, Burton is drawn to the lit domed greenhouse. He stops to rest at a bandstand where he admires the magnificent building reflecting on the pond, creating an eerie double image. At the entrance to the conservatory Burton sees Will's horse.

The sound of rolling thunder causes Burton to spin around to see three horses charging toward him.

Solomon and his sons arrive, each armed, each wearing a gold mask that highlights their eyes and gives the feeling that they are piercing into his soul.

"You're on thin ice!" Solomon says muffled behind his gold mask.

"We told you to take care of Mr. Quillo." Hollis says pointing his rifle at Burton.

"I'm sorry! God help me, I'm sorry. I…I thought Will could help find your property. Which *he* did! There inside the conservatory. At this very moment!"

Solomons gaze is fixed on the enclosed Eden. "Hollis, you, and Mr. Burton sneak in through the front entrance. Israel, I want you to take a defensive position on the other side. Make sure they don't escape! I'll take the high ground."

CHAPTER TEN

Will finishes making Jack's splint. "If you don't' mind me asking, what are you?"

"I am an aquastor," Jack said, "A being summoned into existence by human thought. You see, I am the result of a prank inflicted upon London England by an Irish Nobleman the Marquess of Waterford. A man who, with the help of fellow aristocrats, would dress up and spring on travelers. I am nothing more than a practical joke that got out of control. Soon the whole world was afraid of the leaping demon or as I was better known-"

"Spring-heeled Jack." Will finishes.

"Precisely! I was manifested into existence around the 1840s due to the mass hysteria of thoughts by humans."

"Manifested?"

"You humans have God-like abilities. You forgot how to use them. Each thought in your mind has weight like that of a grain of sand. One grain is nothing. However, when the whole world thinks about the same thing, you have a beach full of sand. I manifested from human thought. I only exist if the world believes in me. Through humanity's combined belief in me, I came into existence. But if you humans forget about me, I will fade away. For my survival, I come out of hiding to remind you lot I'm still here. Hence, the theatrics tonight. I meant no one harm. I am one of the hundreds of bastard children humans have manifested out of fear and anxiety."

"Why do you need the gold chest?"

"That is the second reason why I am here." Jack struggles to hold up the golden chest. "It's called a Rostau chest and can be dangerous in the wrong hands. This sacred relic must be returned. The Masons belong to a secret society called the Brotherhood of Khonsu. I am not aware as to the level of knowledge they possess about this relic, but, with enough time and resources, they could figure it out. Therefore, I have offered my services to help retrieve it."

"Who do you work for?"

"Honestly, the less you know, the safer—"

The sound of gravel crunching in the distance causes both Jack and Will to become alert and silent.

"Don't move!" Burton shouts.

Will looks to see Burton and a stranger wearing a gold Egyptian mask stepping through a grove of hedges.

"Thank you, Mr. Quillo for finding my property. I'll be having that back now."

"Evening Burton. Will says. "And I want to say... Hollis Mason?"

"Jesus!" Burton says gawking at the demon.

Hollis shoulders his rifle. With his free hand he reaches out for Quillo to surrender the gold chest to him. "Nice and slow, Mr. Quillo."

Will takes the gold Rostau chest from Jack and slowly rises.

"Tell me that thing is not real?!" Burton says.

"Stay calm, Mr. Burton. Just keep him under your sights." Hollis says stepping forward to snatch the Rostau chest from Will.

"Will, no!" Jack pleads crawling forward.

"Jack stop!" Will steps in front of Jack, "Burton why are you helping them?"

"I'm sorry, Will."

"Okay, Mr. Burton. Kill them!" Hollis commands casually.

Burton, perspiring in his suit, applied his finger to the trigger.

Will and Burton lock eyes.

"Sam, please don't do this." Will begs. "The Masons are going to *kill you*! If not now, then whenever they don't need you anymore."

"Kill them, Burton. Shoot them in the head."

A gunshot is fired, followed by a spray of blood on Wills face.

Hollis screams as he falls sideways into the gravel.

The gold chest skids towards Jack, who scoops it up into his arms.

Burton moves to stand over Hollis. His pistol shaking in his hand.

Another shot is fired. Only this time from high above. The bullet enters Burtons right eye and exits the back of his neck. His body slumps to the ground.

Will feels a prickly wave of tension wash over his body. He instantly wants to rush to help Burton, but logic takes over as he knows he has only moments before the next shot is fired. And this time it will be at him. He moves behind Jack and hands him his pistol. "Know how to use this?"

"Yes," Jack replies, taking aim where the shot was fired. He sees an armed man up on a widows walk that runs the length of the conservatory. He aims to fire, but Will grabs him from under his arms and drags him away. Jack screams in agony as a red trail of his blood streams out of him.

Bullets rain down barely missing both the officer and the thief.

Hollis rises nursing his left arm. He picks up his pistol and removes his gold mask. He moves through a thicket of olive trees, then steps out to an open area. He finds Jack's blue fire throwing device. Picking it up, Hollis drops it as his hand sears with pain. In a fit of anger, he kicks it away—the device hisses, followed by a howl. Blue flames belch out, and the device shoots like a rocket across the conservatory. The rockets journey ends when it crashes into a gas line that feeds the lamps, causing an explosive wave across the glass dome.

Hollis, now trapped in a ring of fire, cries out for help.

One by one, gas lights explode, popping like fireworks.

The American flag is quickly engulfed in flames.

Outside on the conservatory's roof, Solomon, armed with his Winchester, has moved halfway out over a widow's walk. He pauses to remove his gold mask. Solomon navigates the platform as flames erupt below. Moving to the ladder, he pauses when he spots Officer Quillo, picking up a small boulder. He watches as Quillo throws the boulder through a glass panel, shattering it to pieces.

After clearing away the broken shards of glass, Will returns to help Jack.

A bullet strikes Will, sending him backwards into a grove of marigolds.

"Will!" Jack screams, crawling towards his savior.

Leaning out over the rail, Solomon smiles. He cocks the rifle lever and takes aim at the horned creature. But before he can pull the trigger, an explosion shakes the entire edifice.

Outside the conservatory, Israel watches as fire races through the gas line to its main holding tank. Once the flames enter the tank, it explodes into a giant fire ball that can be seen for miles.

Israel is blown backwards from the blast.

The glass wall on the side of the explosion shatters inward sending glass shards down upon the panicking souls below.

Solomon braces himself before the walkway collapses under the detonation.

Hollis runs, weaving through burning plants to escape the falling metal beams. He pauses in a clearing before dancing around as fire consumes his body. His screams of agony cry out over the flames that lick the air above him.

Solomon lands with the widow's walk. His head smashes into a gravel path.

Israel enters searching for his family. He stumbles around the steel frame house and pauses when he sees his brother Hollis pass through flames only to stop at the sight of their father lying motionless.

Hollis and Israel grab their father and drag his burnt corpse out threw the main entrance.

Once outside, Hollis turns back to scan the fiery inferno for any survivors. "William Quillo! If your still alive, I will get you for this! You and your whole family will pay! Do you hear me?!"

Jack and Will lay in the bed of flowers like dry timber, waiting to be engulfed by the blaze.

"Wake up!" Jack cries, shaking Will.

Will's eyes flutter as he draws a deep breath into his burning lungs. The smell of thick smoke and the feeling of intense heat causes him to bolt upright.

"Oh, thank the stars!" Jack says.

"Ahh!" Will screams as hot blood pours from a deep hole in his shoulder.

The raging fire encircles them.

Will struggles to stand as the room spins around him. He chokes on the smoke as he attempts to move Jack. "I don't have enough strength."

Jack holds the gold relic up to Will. "Leave me!" he cries.

"No!" Will says.

"There's no time! Take it and go! Keep it safe."

Will snatches the golden chest.

Jack holds the pistol to his temple. "Now go!"

There is no time to argue. Will stumbles backward toward the broke-out window. As he turns to leave, he struggles as his legs are as heavy as iron weights.

Outside, Will extinguishes flames that dance up his pants. His attention is brought back to the ruins by the sound of a gunshot.

Will pauses in sorrow.

The moment of reflection ends by the sound of whistles shrilling out, high-pitched calls mixed with the tolling of a bell.

Moments later, Will rides his horse east across Weisinger Avenue and pauses at Fourth Street crossing. Looking north he sees lanterns swaying from fire brigades galloping south toward the raging fire. Will knows the men coming could stop his leaking life, but there is no time. The relic's return is of higher priority.

CHAPTER ELEVEN

Midnight approaches as the half-full moon moves directly overhead, throwing a sleepy yet watchful milky eye upon the earth.

Will rides his horse south down Fourth Street trying to keep himself awake. He feels his pants damp with the life he is leaking. He listens to the song of crickets as he passes flat farmlands, pastures, and fields.

It was then that Will notices a small ball forming in the back of his throat as it occurs to him what field he is passing.

The farm belongs to the House of Refuge, a child prison, and an area Will knows all too well. To this day, this land has the power to make Will feel like a lost child.

Will's father was murdered by angry protesters during the "Bloody Monday" riot of 1855. What was supposed to be a peaceful election day in Louisville that day quickly turned to scenes of violence, bloodshed, and immigrant house burnings. In total, twenty-two people died that day while hundreds of others were wounded.

Will was left to fend for himself and his mother. When he was caught stealing, he became a ward of the state. His mother would die shortly after.

Memories of working these fields rush back to him. This night seems to be awakening all the darkest memories of his past.

The rise of juvenile delinquency in the 1850s forced the city to find a new property large enough to house and work children. This land was ideal for such a facility. It was miles away from the bustling city and provided plenty of space to grow. The goal was to help reform the children of their criminal ways while also providing them experience working in a chosen trade. Younger children worked in laundries, shoe shops, and sewing rooms. Older children were tasked with working the gardens, farmlands, and greenhouses.

Will's internment came long before the campus was built. It was his sweat and blood that forged the grounds for generations of children to follow him. Before the property was transferred to the House of Refuge, the land belonged to the defunct Oakland Cemetery. At the age of ten, young William Quillo's first assignment was to help dig up the deceased and reinter them at Cave Hill Cemetery. At age fifteen, Will enlisted in the Union Army and left the grounds vowing never to return.

Will catches his hand trembling as he suppresses the memory of the smell of rot and decay. The memory of putrid smells causes the ball in his throat to swell and move to the top of his head, making him dizzy. Will fights back the urge to vomit. Instead, he sucks in the air he had forgotten to breathe.

The forest opens to a mass clearing. Fourth Street splits off in two directions. Between the fork in the

CHAPTER ELEVEN

road stands an ad sign depicting a green man's head with a black Egyptian beard and white atef crown, smoking a pipe. The green man is Osiris, the God of fertility, the afterlife, and resurrection. In bold letters, the ad reads, "BU WIZZER, THE CHOICE OF RACETRACK ROYALTY!"

Will halts at the fork. He sees that the road to his left leads past a topiary garden, where a grove of shrubs cut to look like African animals line the road toward the Zoological Garden. The road to his right leads to the silhouette of the racetrack grandstand and betting shed of the Louisville Jockey Club and Driving Park. The grandstand is an open seating area with an awning to cover the 3,500 seats of the multi-level terraces.

Will swallows hard, trying to summon saliva to his dry mouth. He sees darkness for a moment. His eyes are heavier now. Will moves past the grandstand to access the open-aired racetrack, where he discovers a massive cigar-shaped balloon that hovers low above the center field. A lantern lights the suspended gondola below and a figure of a man.

Will sucks in a deep victorious breath of night air before riding up to the hull of the airship. As he nears, he sees the word, *Aquila,* painted on the bow of the gondola. "Hello!" he yells up.

A man dressed in a black leather suit with goggles and black flowing hair appears over the haul. The aeronaut aims his rifle down at Will. "Who are you!?"

"Olvil… Ah… Jack sent me to give you this," Will says, using all his might to hand the Rostau chest up to the aeronaut.

The aeronaut drops his aim and greedily snatches up the holy relic. He carefully examines it before leaning back over to ask, "And where is my associate, Mr. Olvilvicera?"

"I'm sorry, but he's… he's dead."

The aeronaut looks north to see white smoke rising above the tree line. "You've done the right thing," He withdraws a pouch from within his coat pocket and tosses it down.

Will catches the pouch. Whatever is inside has a great deal of weight.

"I must go! Open the pouch! Hold the item inside tight! You'll be alright." The aeronaut gives a salute and steps away from view.

Will opens the heavy pouch and withdraws a seven-inch long golden amulet of a cross with a loop above the T shape. He holds the relic by the base with both hands.

Moments later, the ship slowly ascends to the stary sky above. The propellers begin to rotate, returning to that familiar screeching sound that Will had heard only a few hours earlier that day when this airship first arrived in his city.

Will's gaze stays with the flying ship, watching it rise into the crisp early morning air, rotate west, sail past the moon, and disappear over the black rolling hills of Kentucky.

The moment passes like a dream.

"Mary." he mumbles.

Will's head throbs as the world around him vibrates. The unique cross slips from his pale, numb fingers. His

CHAPTER ELEVEN

head and eyelids become too heavy to bare. Will leans forward, falls off his horse, and sinks deep into the earth, entering a great black watery void.

CHAPTER TWELVE

"Death is swallowed up in light."
—BOOK OF THE MASTER

THE RIVER MEHET-WERET
LOCATED IN THE DUAT *(Realm of the Dead)*
12:12 A.M.

Wills eyelids flutter open as he draws fresh, crisp air into his lungs. In his right hand, he holds the gold cross with a loop. The cross glows a soft gold hue. Inspecting his surroundings, he sees that he is seated on a boat with red sails. His mouth falls open when his gaze moves to the shoreline.

Drifting past him is a dozen pyramids that radiate a variety of colors in the dark of night. He stands in awe and moves to the front of the barge's bow where he discovers a blindfolded woman dressed in a white gown with flowing red hair and bull horns that protrude from the top of her head. Between her horns is a gold disk. A transparent blue ghost-like snake flickers out of her forehead.

"Where… am I?" Will asks.

The woman remains silent as the head of the transparent blue snake tilts to its side.

Will notes his surroundings and sees that no one else is aboard the drifting craft. Despite no one at the helm, the barge is steered into a harbor. The boat moves past docks that connect to causeways leading to different pyramids on a rocky hill.

The barge stops at a causeway leading up to a colossal statue of a reclining lioness that lays surrounded by water. Its stern eyes stare down at the river with a look of foreboding. Behind it three of the largest pyramids in the complex rise like mountains.

Above the pyramids is a dome of stars that fill the sky as far as the eye can see and a wide-eyed full moon.

The horned woman arcs her arm, pointing to the lioness.

"You want me to go… up there?"

She bows her head.

Will steps off the barge and makes his way up the white stone incline. He sees the water lap to the shore where closed lotus flowers bob. His presence activates the buds to open, revealing bright blue, glowing petals.

Will tries to gather his senses. *Am I dead?* he thinks.

In the east, the cloak of darkness is cut by amber from the rise of a new dawn.

At the top, standing between the mighty double paws of the lioness, Will looks back to the boat where the blindfolded, horned woman remains pointing him onward.

At the doorway carved in the chest of the lioness, a stone staircase leads down into darkness. As Will descends the staircase the gold cross brightens in the dark. He descends into an underground chamber that opens into a second larger, circular chamber. At the center of the room is a circular stone altar. A gold chest, like the one he took from Jack and gave to the aeronaut, rests upon the altar.

The gilded Rostau chest fades away.

A flash of light reveals to him another doorway to his right.

Will steps into the new chamber, holding the lit ankh above his head to illuminate the whole room. Taking small steps inside, he looks corner to corner for any signs of danger. At the center of this chamber is another stone altar that holds a stone tablet. A beam of morning sunlight filters down from a square opening from the ceiling creating a luminous haze around the stone alter.

Will steps forward into the haze to better see the text inscribed upon the ancient tablet.

He reads,

> *Hope is the only good god remaining among mankind;*
> *the others have left and gone to Olympus.*
> *Trust, a mighty god has gone, restraint has gone from men,*
> *and the Graces, my friend, have abandoned the earth.*
> *Men's judicial oaths are no longer to be trusted,*
> *nor does anyone revere the immortal gods;*
> *the race of pious men has perished,*
> *and men no longer recognize the rules of conduct*
> *or acts of piety.*

-THEOGNIS of MEGARA

Pondering over the ancient text's meaning, Will feels deep within himself a calling to remain a good man.

Will you stay true to yourself? His subconscious asks.

CHAPTER TWELVE

Yes! Will answers.

Another light erupts, revealing yet another chamber. The chamber is illuminated with a gold aura of light.

Will hesitates before moving to this threshold. He can fill the energy coming from within the joint chamber. He senses no danger. Only a sense of goodness. The feeling one gets when entering a church or temple. Breathing heavier now, Will enters the portal and sees an auditorium full of mythical creatures, human beings, and supernatural beings made of light.

Will feels his mind empty of all thought with a deep sense of connection to all those around him. Although he is cut off from the world he knows, he feels oddly at peace here. Breathing out, Will senses the darkness that has lingered with him now gone. The feeling of being a "lost child" vanishes.

Breathing deeply, the hole in William Quillo's heart becomes whole.

An old forgotten sensation courses through his body. One that he has not felt since childhood.

Tears of joy stream down his face.

The horned woman approaches. Her body is glowing with an intense aura of light. Raising her hands, Will is gently lifted into the air.

With a look of horror, Will floats upward as he struggles to understand his means of flight.

The light swallows him.

SPRING-ꞪEELED JACK

LOUISVILLE HOSPITAL
LOCATED AT CHESTNUT & FLOYD STREET

Slipping back into consciousness, Will awakens laying on his back on a hard mattress.

Daylight pours in through a row of windows.

As he moves his hand to block out the light, it is jerked back by a silver handcuff that binds him to the hospital bed.

Feeling no pain, he sees that his wound has completely healed with no trace of a scar. His eyes narrow as his mind still tapers between worlds. *Why am I cuffed?*

Through the window of a door, he can see an armed guard standing at attention. His memory rushes back to him. *Jack! "The Masons!"*

Bathed in light, prisoner 777 fiercely struggles against his restraints.

"Oh, no! No!" Will cries.

To be continued...

William Quillo will return in,

THE BROTHERHOOD OF KHONSU
or
THE TERROR OF LOUISVILLE
PART II

THE GREAT EXPOSITION

I would like to address the claim that my story, *Spring-heeled Jack or The Terror of Louisville Part 1,* is based on true events.

Here are the facts:
All descriptions of architecture, and artwork in this short story are accurate. In fact, many locations mentioned in this story are real and still exist to this day. I invite readers to travel to Louisville and see these locations in person.

The Freemasons – a fraternal organization and secret society. Its founding is unknown. The most widely accepted theory is that they began as stonemasons guides of the Middle Ages and possible influenced by the Knights Templar. Their most sacred belief is making the world a better place to live for all people. Famous members include George Washington, Benjamin Franklin, Oscar Wilde, Harry Houdini, Wolfgang Amadeus Mozart, Mark Twain and many more.

THE GREAT EXPOSITION

Freemasons have been in Louisville for over 200 years.

The Constellations on the front cover of the book are historical accurate to what the night sky looked like on the evening of July 28th, 1880.

The Demon Leaper – Was Spring-heeled Jack in Louisville? The only piece of evidence of a demon leaper in Louisville comes from investigative reporter, Jim Brandon from his book *Weird America: A Guide To Places Of Mystery In The United States* (1978). In his book he reports that around July 1880 a "tall and thin weirdo" began to attack Louisville residents. Eyewitnesses describe the creature as being "agile as a monkey and with a long nose, pointed ears, and long fingers" he continues, "On his chest under the cape was a large, bright light and his favorite method of escape was to spring smoothly over high objects." This evidence was also cited in author Jeffrey Scott Holland's *Weird Kentucky* and David Dominé's *Haunts of Old Louisville*.

The Aerial Mystery – On July 28th, 1880, in Louisville, Kentucky a flying machine was seen passing over the city. It was reported to the *Courier-Journal* newspaper. I found the article from the Free Public Library located on York Street in downtown Louisville. I have also provided in this book a picture of that news article.

RIDLEY BARNETT

MORE MONKEYING

Between the Talented Reporters and That Well-preserved Old Dame, Madame Rumor.

A Flying Machine Which Two Louisvillians Saw Passing Over the City.

A Queer Attempt at Suicide—A Husband Who is Non Est—A Female Drunkard in Court.

WITH OTHER EDIFYING MORSELS OF NEWS.

A FLYING MACHINE.

WHAT TWO LOUISVILLIANS SAW LAST EVENING.

Between 6 and 7 o'clock last evening while Messrs. C. A. Youngman and Ben Fleamer were standing at a side window of Haddart's drug store, at Second and Chestnut streets, looking skyward, they discovered an object high up in the air apparently immediately above the Ohio river bridge, which they at first thought was the wreck of a toy balloon. As it got nearer they observed that it had the appearance of a man surrounded by machinery, which he seemed to be working with his feet and hands. He worked his feet as though he was running a treadle, and his arms seemed to be swinging to and fro above his head, though the latter movement sometimes appeared to be exercised with wings or fans. The gases became considerably worked up by the apparition, and inspected it very closely. They could see the delicate outlines of machinery, but the object was too high up to make out the exact construction. At times it would seem to be descending, and then the man appeared to exert himself considerably, and ran the machine faster, when it would ascend again and assume a horizontal position. It did not travel as fast as a paper balloon, and its course seemed to be entirely under the control of the aeronaut. At first it was traveling in a southeastward direction, but when it reached a point just over the city, it turned and went due south, until it had passed nearly over the city, when it tacked to the southwest, in which direction it was going when it passed out of sight in the twilight of the evening. The gentlemen who saw it are confident that it was a man navigating the air on a flying-machine. His movements were regular, and the machine was under the most perfect control. If he belonged to this mundane sphere he should have dropped his card as he passed over, to enlighten those who saw him, and that his friends, if he has any, might be informed of his whereabouts.

Courier-Journal's July 29th, 1880, article about the Flying Machine.

THE GREAT EXPOSITION

Fictional Characters - William Quillo is based on real life Louisville detective, Delos Bligh. The Mason family are not real. Thank God! However, I based Hollis Mason on Louisville crime boss John Henry Whallen and English occultist and ceremonial magician, Aleister Crowley.

Non-fictional Characters – Robert Fox, a friend of William Quillo. Fox's background information given in *Spring-heeled Jack* is historical accurate. As well as Mayor Baxter, a character whose appearance is only mentioned. His attempted assassination by Robert Redd did in fact happen.

I hope this article brings some clarity to those who are curious about the true events of my short story. When reading the genre of historical fiction readers want to be swept away to a time long past. Readers yearn to have the old world come alive on each page. With historical figures, fictional characters, historical settings, and a fictional plot *Spring-heeled Jack or The Terror of Louisville Part I* helps readers to better understand the past and hopefully bring clarity about events happing in the present.

-Ridley Barnett
July 4th,2023

AUTHOR'S MESSAGE

There are many aspects to the short story, *Spring-heeled Jack or The Terror of Louisville Part 1*, that readers should study carefully. This exciting historical fiction adventure is designed to engage readers to rethink their understanding of the universe and our place in it. With each new episode, readers will be guided into this esoteric world to help draw from it the means to change the world for the better.

To help give clarity to some of the more unknown elements of this book, an encyclopedia has been provided to help better understand important persons, places, and things.

May this knowledge elevate you to a new level of consciousness.

So Mote It Be!

ENCYCLOPEDIA

AIRSHIP. Hot Air Balloons have been around since 1709. The first airship or dirigible balloon was invented in 1851. In 1852 Henri Giffard created the first steam-powered airship. The advanced airship that was seen flying over the skies of Louisville, Kentucky, in 1880 would not be seen again for another ten years.

AMEN. From the Egyptian word, Amun that means "to keep hidden."

DEMON LEAPER of LOUISVILLE. Native American legends and early European settlers have been reporting stories of strange, winged creatures haunting the Ohio Valley area for some time. Today there have been multiple reports of a leaping demon on the roof of the Walnut Street Baptist Church.

GLOBAL MIND. Noetic Science studies intellectual and spiritual capabilities such as self-healing and telepathy. One of the projects that Noetic Science researchers' study is Global Consciousness. Imagine that all humans on Earth are connected to transmit feelings and ideas across the globe with their mind. In *Spring-heeled Jack or The Terror of Louisville Part 1*, Jack explains to Police Officer William Quillo that humans have "god-like abilities." Jack was manifested into existence by way of a Global Mind.

ENCYCLOPEDIA

IRISH IMMIGRANTS. Between 1820 and 1860, the Irish made up one-third of all immigrants to the United States. In 1801 Ireland was ruled as a colony by Great Britain. Many Irish immigrated to America after many of their crops and goods were taken by Great Britain. By 1845 the Irish Potato Famine struck, causing an increase in immigration to the United States.

KHEMIT. "Black Land". (Egypt). This name is what the indigenous and the ancients used to describe Egypt. During the annual summer flooding of the Nile, rich black alluvial soil would nourish its banks. This dark soil would help fuel the growth of the crops. The people of Khemit were called Sesh.

LOUISVILLE. Founded in 1778 by George Rogers Clark, it is the largest city in the Commonwealth of Kentucky. The city was named in honor of King Louis XVI of France and is one of the oldest towns west of the Appalachians.

LOUISVILLE JOCKEY CLUB. A horse racing complex famed for hosting the Kentucky Derby. Today it is known as Churchill Downs. Founded in 1875 and named after Samuel Churchill.

PYRAMIDS. According to the Khemitian tradition, the pyramids were initially called Per-Bas (house of spirit) and Per-Neters (house of nature/energy). The purpose of a Per-Ba was to help raise the consciousness of initiates while Per-Neters were used to generate energy.

ENCYCLOPEDIA

ROSTAU. Meaning "mouth of the passages" was the ancient Khemitian (Egyptian) name for the Giza Plateau. This area sits on the outskirts of Cairo, Egypt, and is known today as an ancient Necropolis. The site includes the Great Pyramid of Khufu, Khafre, Menkaure, and the Sphinx.

ROSTAU CHEST. The gold chest sought after by the Mason family and Spring-heeled Jack is a fictitious relic that was inspired by the ancient Egyptian hieroglyph of the House of the Rostau. This ancient house acts as a doorway to the ancient Egyptian underworld.

SPHINX. According to Khemitian tradition, the Sphinx is 52,000 years old. Her name is Tefnut, and she represents the sky or the feminine consciousness of space. Tefnut represents Sekhmet, Men-Het, and Mut. Her name translates to "The Spittle of Nut" and was the first physical manifestation upon Earth.

SPRING-HEELED JACK. The first documented sighting of Spring-heeled Jack was in 1837 in London, England. Over the next several years, the sighting of the demon leaper was reported around the world. There are many theories to explain the strange appearance of the demon leaper. The most accepted theory is of a gang of young men with well-connected families disguised to perform practical jokes upon a gullible public.

ENCYCLOPEDIA

TOBACCO. According to the Saskatchewan Indian Center, the most powerful way to communicate with the spirit world is to smoke tobacco. All around the world in every culture burring incenses is thought to bring down heavenly beings. Tobacco is used often throughout the Terror of Louisville books.

APPINDIX

Source of Maps

Bancroft & Company, A. L. "Map of the City of Louisville,
>Ky. *International Office, and Family Atlas of the World.* Call Number: A1.A1 1890. KY1." *The Barnett Library*, [Louisville]: Barnett Private Library, [1890].

Breckinridge. "Index Map of the City of Louisville, Ky. Call Number: G3954.L7 1879. K4." *The Library of Congress*, [Louisville]: The Association, [1879?], www.loc.gov/resource.com.

Lionel Pincus and Princess Firyal Map Division, The New York Public Library. "The Caron map of the city of Louisville" *The New York Public Library Digital Collections*. 1880. https://digitalcollections.nypl.org/items/3f106830-3d76-0135-bce7-09ed97aa7b8a

BIBLIOGRAPHY

Crews, Clyde F. "Second Street." *In Crossings: Historical Journeys Near Louisville's Merton Square*, Louisville, KY: Bellarmine University Press, 2009, p. 37.

Dominé, David. "Chapter 3: The Walnut Street Baptist Church." *Haunts of Old Louisville: Gilded Age Ghosts and Haunted Mansions in America's Spookiest Neighborhood*, University Press of Kentucky, 2017, pp. 70–76.

Holland, Jeffery Scott. "Strange Phenomena." *Weird Kentucky: Your Travel Guide to Kentucky's Local Legends and Best Kept Secrets,* New York: Sterling Pub, 2008, p. 58-59.

Kleber, John E. "House of Refuge," "Phoenix Hill," "Bloody Monday Riot," "The Falls of Ohio," "Broadway," "Louisville Jockey Club & Driving Park." *The Encyclopedia of Louisville*, The University Press of Kentucky, 2015, p. 406, 701, 97, 279, 129, & 181.

Mehler S. Stephen, "Khemitology – New Paradigms" & "Giza" *The Land of Osiris*, Adventures Unlimited Press, 2001, p. 48-49 & 116.

BIBLIOGRAPHY

Mullin, Timothy J. "The du Ponts in Kentucky:
    Louisville's Central Park, the Southern
    Exposition, and an Entrepreneurial Spirit."
    Western Kentucky University, 21 Sept. 2019, p.
    21 – 29.

Riebel, R. C., "1880." *Louisville Panorama: A Visual
    History of Louisville*, Liberty National Bank &
    Trust Company, 1960, p. 108.

Thomas, Samuel W. "du Pont Family's Central Park
    (1872)," & "Louisville Park Initiatives (1880s)."
    The Origins of Louisville's Olmsted Parks &
    Parkways, 1st ed., Holland Brown Books, 2013,
    p. 84–85, & p. 107-108.

WORK CITED

Theognis of Megara, "Pandora's Box." 6th Century BD, Greece.

NEXT PAGE *PUBLISHERS*

For More Exciting Books
& Upcoming Events, Visit Us At
WWW.NEXTPAGEPUBLISHERS.COM

Read Another Great Story
From RIDLEY BARNETT

TWO STEPS
FROM HELL
ORIGINAL SCREENPLAY

**A FRIGHTNING AND POWERFUL TALE of
One Man's Journey Through The Afterlife!**

The Henu Express, a locomotive that transports
the recently deceased, crosses Duat, the land of the
dead, to deliver its passengers to their final destination.

John Phoenix awakes on board the Henu Express,
unaware that he is dead, and discovers he is bound for
Perdition. Jumping from the train, John journeys to
find clues to his past. Along the way, he must evade the
Medjay, guardians of the Netherworld, and demons
that seek his help.

If John succeeds, will he escape with a new life or be
damned forever in the fiery pits of Hell?

COMING SOON

**Read on for an excerpt from
TWO STEPS FROM HELL**

BLACK SCREEN.

TITLE:

DEATH IS JUST THE BEGINNING…

-ANCIENT PROVERB

DISSOLVE TO:

TITLE:

TWO STEPS FROM HELL

FADE IN:

EXT. DESERT – NIGHT (TITLE SEQUENCE
BEGINS)

A full moon hangs high over a desert plateau casting
long shadows across the rocky terrain. Thousands of
stars gleam in the night sky.

In the distance, a massive altostratus cloud, shelflike
in appearance moves swiftly between land and
heaven.

Like a stage curtain closing out a performance, the storm clouds roll over the milky face of the moon and sparkling night sky.

A heavy downpour hits the desert.

A lone light beam from a passenger train pierces through the darkness.

WE MOVE TOWARD THE RAIL VEHICLE.

The train snakes its way through the desert at high speed.

VIEW FROM BEHIND THE TRAINS CHIMNEY.

The train crosses over a bridge. Its whistle sounds off two long blasts followed by one short and one long.

CLOSE UP OF THE DRIVING WHEEL, CRANK, AND CONNECTING ROD ROTATING FURIOUSLY.

CUT TO:

AT THE REAR OF THE TRAIN, WE PASS THROUGH THE WINDOWPANE.

INT. PASSENGER CAR - STORMY NIGHT
WE MOVES UP THE AISLE PASSING…

The car is packed with travelers of all ages. Many people are reading and studying from a black book.

Some riders pray quietly while others sob uncontrollable.

The only source of light comes from lanterns that sway above the aisle causing shadows to dance around the cabin.

WE CONTINUE TO MOVE FROM ONE RAIL CAR AND INTO THE NEXT. THERE IS REPETITION OF EVENTS IN EACH CAR. WE CONTINUE UNTIL WE REACH THE FRONT COMPARTMENT.

The mood shifts at the front passenger car. Here the riders are smiling and laughing. They are all dressed in white clothing.

Beer and bread are offered to the travelers by a servant dressed in a red uniform.

CAMERA PASSES SEAT AFTER SEAT UNTIL IT REACHES A MAN WHO IS ASLEEP.

CREDIT SEQUENCE ENDS WITH:
TITLE:

EPISODE I:

THE HENU BARK EXPRESS

The sleeping man's arms are crossed, head down, as his brown fedora hides his face. This is John Phoenix, a thirty-three-year-old American man.

The other passengers stand and begin to sing.

SONG: "I'M GOING HOME" BY SACRED
HARP SINGERS AT LIBERTY CHURCH.

John is awakened by the sudden commotion. He sits
up with a confused look upon his face. He is wearing
a light blue shirt with suspenders. He is a mess
compared to everyone else in the car.

The entire rail car is full of people singing with joy as
they pound their feet and clap to the rhythm of the
hymn's melody.

SINGING GROUP

Come, come now were going home, home, home.

Outside his window is only darkness. A bolt of
lightning cracks the atmosphere.

John searches his pants pockets. Nothing. He
searches his shirt pocket and finds a train ticket. He
reads from the ticket; One way passage to
PERDITION.

JOHN (V.O.)

What the Hell?

A dark shadow is cast over John.

COACH ATTENDANT
(standing beside John)

Sir, I believe that you're in the wrong car! Follow me
please.

JOHN
(standing up wide eyed)
There's been a mistake. I don't remember getting on——-

ATTENDANT
(snatching John's ticket)
You are…
(reading the ticket)
…John Alister Phoenix?

JOHN (V.O.)
(look of confusion)
My name is...?

ATTENDANT
(thumbing to the rear)
There is one mistake!
You're supposed to be in the rear. With the others.

INT. REAR OF THE TRAIN - CONTINUOUS

Walking into the next railcar, John notes the dramatic change in tone and mood. Back here travelers are miserable.

After walking halfway through the length of the iron snake, The Coach Attendant stops at an empty seat.

JOHN
(concerned)
Where is Perdition? Utah? Where are we now?

RIDLEY BARNETT

ATTENDANT
(handing back the ticket)
Trying to be funny, are ya? Take yo seat. And try not
to lose this.

JOHN
(to the Coach Attendant)
Is this ticket one way or is it also a return? I don't
know if I'll have enough money to get back home.

ATTENDANT

Sit down!

John sits as the Coach Attendant grunts in annoyance
as he walks back up the aisle shaking his head in
disapproval.

John closes his eyes and takes a deep breath. He tries
to remember the last thing he did before he went to
sleep. Before he boarded this train.

JOHN (V.O.)
(scratching his chin)
How the hell did I get here?

Nothing.

John notices that the seats in this car are like church
pews. They even have a book cradle mounted behind
each seat. Curious, he pulls a black book from its
cradle. In golden letters, its title reads, THE BOOK
OF COMING FORTH BY DAY. 5,173rd edition. In

parentheses below the subtitle reads, A BOOK FOR THE DEAD.

Lightning outside illuminates the cabin.

John flips through the book's pages, stopping to examine each of the black and white illustrated drawings.

Images of people walking into paradise.

Images of people buried with their heads sticking out of a cave floor.

> JOHN

What in tarnation?

LIGHTNING FLASHES.

Skipping to the middle of the book John sees an illustration that sends a chill down his back. A tower is being carried by bald, naked humanoids across a vast empty desert. Ridding atop of the tower is a horned devil, clothed only by a cape that waves in the sky. A flock of raven's form an unholy crown above the gothic tower.

A flash of lighting follows a low rumble of thunder.

John closes the book and scans the passenger car for someone of authority.

PASSENGER #1
(Spanish accent)
Well, not too much longer until we reach our destination. Nervous?

The voice comes from behind John. This is Edwardo, a man in his late 50's. He is wearing an all-gray three-piece suit topped with a black bowler hat.

JOHN
(turning around)
Yeah well, I'm not sure exactly where Perdition is on a map, but I know I don't want to go there.

EDWARDO
(extends his hand)
Ha! That's a good one. Keeping a sense of humor, I see. Well, that's good. I'm Edwardo Sands, and you are Señor?

JOHN
(shaking hands)
My name is... Ah...

John looks at the name on his ticket.

JOHN
Sorry... John. John Phoenix

EDWARDO
(putting on glasses)
Forgot your name?

JOHN
(rubbing his head)
Honestly, I am having trouble remembering anything.

EDWARDO
(social laugh)
Stress can do that.

JOHN
When is the next stop? I need to transfer back to...
wherever I'm from.

EDWARDO
(puzzled)
Señor?

JOHN
I'm a little embarrassed. You see I don't remember
getting on a train and...

EDWARDO
(concerned)
Señor, do you not know where you are? Do you not
know what's happened?

JOHN
(confused)
Uh... well no sir, you see-

                    EDWARDO
                    (shocked)
Señor, you're on a train to Hell!

Silence a beat.

                    EDWARDO
                (over his shoulder)
Attendant! Is there a coach attendant nearby?

John notes everyone's attention is drawn to Edwardo.

                     JOHN
                 (getting up)
I need some air.

                    EDWARDO
Señor, you need to sit down!

John moves out into the aisle.

                     JOHN
I'm in no mood for games! I want to get home! I want
to go...

                MALE PASSENGER #1
                 (yelling to John)
You're dead, you stupid-son-bitch!

Before John can react to the absurd statement, the
front door of the rail car opens.

A cuffed man rushes inside followed by two other men who snag him for only a moment before he breaks free and runs to the other end of the rail car pushing past John.

PRISONER
(frantic)
I'm not going! You can't make me!

The prisoner opens the back door only to find an explosion of black smoke and howling wind.

John watches in horror as the prisoner is blown backwards. Before landing his body is caught and picked up by the black smoke. He is pulled back to the front of the car.

John leaps back to his seat and watches as the prisoner swims past him through the air surrounded by the black smoke.

The prisoner is swept outside. The doors slam shut.

The compartment goes silent.

JOHN
(terrified)
What the hell was that? What the hell just happened?

MALE PASSENGER #2
(calmly answers)
Runaway!

EDWARDO

There are guardians on the train. They keep anyone from jumping off.

WE MOVE CLOSE ON JOHN WHO turns to look out the window.

EXT. DESERT – CONTINUOUS

The train breaks through the storm....

TWO STEPS FROM HELL
Available Spring 2026

ALSO BY
RIDLEY BARNETT

A JOURNEY INTO DUAT
A SHORT STORY

Hollis Rosenkreuz, a wealthy antique collector, has purchased a peculiar ancient Egyptian gold box to add to his unique collection. Mysteriously, Hollis awakens the following day atop the Great Pyramid of Giza.

The Egyptian gold box has collected him!

Trapped in Cairo, Hollis is forced to journey into the Duat, the ancient Egyptian afterlife, to get back home.

Will Hollis survive the perils of the Netherworld?

FORTHCOMING

Don't Miss The Book That Is Now
A Short Film From
Renegade Art Productions

FOR SALE
BY OWNER
(revised edition)

Short Story & Screenplay
By Keith Barnett Huff

Jeffersonville, Indiana. On the hottest day of the year, John, a man in his thirties, is tasked by his sister to sell their recently deceased parents' van. Unfortunately, the day does not go as planned as John must overcome a colorful array of crazy buyers and his own hesitation to sell the object that connects him to his parents. Will John be able to overcome his grief?

Book & Film
Available on **amazon.com**

ACKNOWLEDMENTS

To my brother Brian and his family, thank you for your continued support.

As always, to my beautiful wife, Grace, your wise words and loving support are a source of strength and the reason I *keep moving forward*.

I want to give a special thanks to my editor, Danielle Kent, whose friendship and editing skills have given me the confidence to release this manuscript after many years of re-writes and self-doubt about this project.

I want to give a very special thanks to playwright and professor Bryan Delaney (*Bailbirds & The Sounding*) and author and professor Christopher Mooney (*The Snow Girls & The Missing*) at Harvard University, who supported and advised me while I was developing this story in their classes.

And finally, a very, very special thanks to Louisville author David Dominé. I first read Mr. Dominé's work at my grandmother's house. She loved ghost stories and had a copy of Dominé's book, *Phantoms of Old Louisville*. Mr. Dominé has written many books about Louisville, Kentucky. I met Mr. Dominé at a book signing event in Old Louisville during the St. James Art

Fair. At the time I was researching this book, he was gracious enough to take the time to answer my questions. After completing the *Spring-heeled Jack or The Terror of Louisville Part I* draft, Mr. Dominé offered to read and write a blurb for my story. And for that, I thank you.

-Ridley Barnett
July 4th,2024

ABOUT THE AUTHOR

RIDLEY BARNETT is an American, philosopher, painter, and novelist. Ridley studied writing and literature at Harvard University. He grew up in Bardstown Kentucky and now lives in Louisville with his wife.

```
         A
        AB
       ABR
      ABRA
     ABRAC
    ABRACA
   ABRACAD
  ABRACADA
 ABRACADAB
ABRACADABR
ABRACADABRA
```

SATOR
AREPO
TENET
OPERA
ROTAS

www.ingramcontent.com/pod-product-compliance
Lightning Source LLC
Chambersburg PA
CBHW022035170626
46808CB00003B/1211